Josh and Dottie McDowell

PIZZA FOR EVERYONE

Illustrated by Meredith Johnson

Chariot Books
David C. Cook Publishing Co.

To Mom and Dad Youd
We speak with our hearts when we
say ``thanks'' for your unending love,
enthusiastic encouragement, faithful
support, and Christ-like example.

Chariot Books is an imprint of David C. Cook Publishing Co.
David C. Cook Publishing Co., Elgin, Illinois 60120
David C. Cook Publishing Co., Weston, Ontario

PIZZA FOR EVERYONE

Book design by Dawn Lauck

First Printing, 1988
Printed in the United States of America
93 92 91 90 89 88   5 4 3 2 1

LIBRARY OF CONGRESS
Library of Congress Cataloging-in-Publication Data
McDowell, Josh.
    Pizza for everyone/Josh and Dottie McDowell; illustrated by
Meredith Johnson.
        p. cm.
    Summary: Amy's first soccer game teaches her that it's how you play,
not whether you win, that counts.
    ISBN 1-55513-596-X
    [1. Soccer—Fiction.   2. Self-acceptance—Fiction.] I. McDowell,
Dottie. II. Johnson, Meredith, ill. III. Title.
PZ7.M478446Pi 1988
[E]—dc19   88-14041
                                                      CIP
                                                       AC

DEAR PARENTS,

You and I have one of the most important responsibilities a person could ever have—caring for and raising a child. And communicating a strong sense of acceptance to our children will go a long way toward developing a healthy sense of self-worth. *Pizza for Everyone*, along with the discussion questions at the end of the story, will help you teach your child that acceptance *is not* based on performance.

Josh and I do our best to communicate our complete acceptance of our children as persons of worth—no matter what they have or have not done. As in the story, a child may not have the talent to be a star soccer player, but as parents we must let the child know that he or she is special to us whether the game is won or lost. For it is *our* acceptance of our children that plays such a vital role in their self-acceptance.

Parenting specialists suggest that children's self-concept is largely determined by what they believe the most important person in their life thinks of them. So we need to be sure our children feel we love and accept them as persons of infinite worth regardless of their grades, musical or athletic abilities, popularity, or anything else.

The importance of a child's self-worth is so evident in the ''WHY WAIT?'' campaign, which prepares young people to say no to premarital sex. Our research shows the more a child feels loved and accepted at home, the less temptation he or she has to seek acceptance or security through a premarital sexual relationship. The foundation of acceptance you lay now, when your child is young, builds a base for his or her moral convictions in years to come.

Yours, for helping our youth,

Dottie McDowell

Amy dashed in the door from school. "Mom!" she called. "Mom! I can be on a soccer team. All you have to do is sign this paper."

Her mom laughed. "Slow down. Give me a chance to find out all about this soccer team." She took the paper Amy was waving at her and sat down to read it.

Amy leaned over the back of her mom's chair. "Please let me be on the team. I've never, *ever* wanted to do something so much. I've got to be on the team," Amy begged.

"Why is playing soccer so important to you?" Mom asked, looking at Amy.

"I *love* soccer. And Mrs. Swanson at school says I'm a good player. But Brandon and Jeff are mean when Mrs. Swanson puts us on the same team. They say soccer is for boys, and I can't run fast enough. At recess, Brandon and Jeff won't let me play. The only girl who plays at recess is Allison."

"Are Brandon and Jeff joining this team, too?" Mom asked.

"I think so. And they can't stop me from being on the team. It says here—boys *and* girls." Amy pointed at the paper her mom held. "I'll show them I'm good enough to play on their team. I'll be the star. Then they'll have to let me play at recess!"

Mom was quiet for a minute. "Playing soccer is fine, and you can join the team. But play because you love the game. Don't try to prove you're the best player—or to make kids like you better. Just play as well as you can. Do your best. That's all Dad and I—and God—expect of you."

Amy threw her arms around her mother's neck. "Oh, thank you! I'll do my best—and I *will* be the star player. I just know it."

Fifteen kids came to the first soccer practice. Brandon and Jeff and Allison were there along with some other kids from Amy's class.

"I'll show them," Amy said to herself. "They'll see that I can be a soccer star. I can't wait for the first game."

Amy loved soccer practice. She worked harder than anyone else.

The drills made her tired, but she also knew they would make her a soccer star if she kept at them.

Finally the big day came. The first game. On the way to the game, Amy's father suggested, ''Let's ask God to help you and the team do your best today. You know, Amy, that's what is really important. Whether the team wins or not—or whether or not you are a star—you're always a champ when you do your best.''

"Okay, Eagles, gather 'round," the coach called. "Here's our starting team: Brandon, Jeff, Allison . . ."

Amy's heart pounded, waiting to hear her name. But the coach didn't even look in her direction. Disappointed, Amy watched from the sidelines as the game began. How could she be a star if she didn't even play?

Loud cheers from her teammates interrupted her thoughts. Allison had scored a goal! Soon Amy was cheering louder than anyone. The game was more exciting than she had imagined, even with the score Beavers 3, Eagles 2.

When the last period began, Amy hoped the coach
would let her play. But he still didn't call her name. She
wondered if she had become invisible.

As the Eagles moved the ball down the field, one of the
Beavers ran in front of Brandon. Both boys went down—
and Brandon stayed on the ground holding his ankle.

The coach looked straight at Amy. ''Okay, Kid, here's
your big chance. You're in for Brandon.''

Amy's heart raced. Her mouth went dry. "Now I'll show everybody," she told herself. She heard the crowd cheer as her first pass was perfect. They were cheering for *her*.

With a minute left in the game, the score was tied. Amy's legs ached from running, but she didn't care. She stole the ball from the Beavers and dribbled toward the goal.

"That-a-way, Champ!" she heard her dad holler. With a mighty kick she sent the ball to Jeff. But a Beaver—not Jeff—suddenly appeared, took the ball, and headed down the field. Amy, Jeff, and all the Eagles took off after him, but no one was fast enough to catch him. As time ran out, the Beavers scored.

Amy couldn't move. How could her pass have missed Jeff? As the team walked slowly off the field, Jeff scowled at Amy. She heard him tell Brandon, "She blew it. Why do girls have to play?"

Before she could hear Brandon's answer, her dad ran up to the team. "Hey, Coach," he yelled. "The team played hard and well. Let's celebrate. Pizza on me!"

"They sure played great—and this was just our first game. Way to go, everyone," the coach answered. "Let's get that pizza!"

As Amy and her dad walked to the car, Dad put his arm around her. "I'm proud of you, Champ. You did a superb job."

Amy couldn't hold back the tears any longer. "How can you say that, Dad? I lost the game. Jeff says I blew it, and probably everyone else thinks so, too."

"Not everyone. Some people may think you're okay only if you win, but Mom and I know you're special whether you win or not."

Dad explained, "The way you practice hard, play hard, and cheer the others on—even when you're not in the game—is what really counts, not the final score.

"And you know what? Right now your dad and your heavenly Father are so proud of you. I'm sure God is smiling ear to ear because you faithfully did your best today."

Amy wiped her eyes as she looked up and smiled. "I'm glad you and Mom are my parents."

"Well, I'm glad God let Mom and me be your parents, Champ!" Dad grinned. "Now, how about that pizza?"

"Sounds good to me," Amy said as she gave him a big hug.

- Why did Amy want to be on the soccer team?

- Would you have blamed Amy for losing the game? Why or why not?

- Why do you think Amy's dad was proud of her?

- What are some things you work hard at—like Amy worked at playing soccer?

- How does Amy know her parents love her? How do you know I love you?